For Hannah and Ian ~ J.D.
For Liz, with love ~ A.C.

First published in 2004 by Macmillan Children's Books
A division of Macmillan Publishers Limited
20 New Wharf Road, London N1 9RR
Basingstoke and Oxford
Associated companies throughout the world
www.panmacmillan.com

ISBN 0 333 94781 9 (HB)
ISBN 0 333 94782 7 (PB)

Text copyright © Julia Donaldson 2004
Illustrations copyright © Anna Currey 2004
Moral rights asserted.

1 3 5 7 9 8 6 4 2 (HB)
1 3 5 7 9 8 6 4 2 (PB)

A CIP catalogue record for this book is available from the British Library.

Printed in Belgium by Proost

One Ted Falls Out of Bed

Julia Donaldson

Illustrated by Anna Currey

MACMILLAN CHILDREN'S BOOKS

One ted
Falls out of bed.

He tugs and pulls the bedclothes BUT . . .

Two eyes are tight shut.

He jumps and shouts and makes a fuss,

Till three mice say, "Play with us!"

They roar around
in four fast cars,

Then sit and gaze at five bright stars.

They sip some tea with six kind dolls

And have a fight with seven trolls.

They take a trip with eight balloons

To where nine frogs are playing tunes.

But one ted
Is missing bed.

Cheer up, Bear,
Build a stair.

One, two, three,   four, five, six,

Seven, eight, nine,
TEN RED BRICKS!

Ted is at the very top
When . . .

Ten bricks crash,
Nine frogs hop,

And eight balloons go
BANG SNAP POP!

Seven trolls start running riot.
Six dolls whisper, "Shush! Be quiet!"
Five stars shine as bright as day.
Four cars hoot and roar away.

Three mice scamper off to hide.

Two eyes open wide,

And one ted . . .

Is back in bed.